Dreams
&
Destiny

BOOKSQUIRREL

Book*Squirrel* Publication

Regd. Under MSME Act.

"Dreams & destiny"

By: Vandana Pamulaparthy

ISBN: 978-93-89557-67-1

Language English

1ˢᵗ Edition

Formatting: Rubal Choudhary

Cover: Ronak

Two roads diverged in a wood, and I—

I took the one less traveled by,

And that has made all the difference.

The Road Not Taken

By Robert Frost

You are the sunshine of our lives

You are the reason of our smiles

To the three little munchkins

Mayank, Sumedh and Harathi

PREFACE

'Dreams & Destiny' is my debut book which is a collection of poetry with varying themes dealing diverse subjects such as nature, life and death to love, rejection, and heartbreak. They are written in simple yet elegant words to convey their meaning to the reader in an appeasing manner.

Based on a relative theme that they share, the poems are categorized into five groups, namely 'Seasons & Sun', 'Love & Lament', 'Illusions & Imagery', 'Life & Legacy' and 'Dark & Desolate' aimed to enthrall and connect with the reader.

Some poems are carved from my own emotions; some are inspired by observation of the world around me and the remaining others are the results of my musings or simply products of my imagination.

Though most of the poems are written in freestyle, I took up a challenge to write in various modern poetic forms which I have included in the appendix.

I put in my best efforts to reach large number of people through simple words and easy to understand language which I hope the reader enjoys.

ACKNOWLEDGEMENTS

Firstly, I am thankful to God for his eternal blessings.

I am immensely grateful to Book Squirrel Publications in making a dream come true. It was a pleasure working with Rubal Choudhary and Mr.Ash.

I am indebted to all the wonderful poets and writers in Instagram for being a source of inspiration as well as constant encouragement to bring out the best in me.

My humble gratitude to my family who has been my pillars of strength at all times holding us together.

Last but not the least; I am thankful to my friends who have been supporting me through this journey as a writer.

ABOUT THE AUTHOR

Vandana holds a post-graduate degree in Pharmaceutics. She worked as an assistant professor before deciding to be a stay-at-home mother.

Writing is a passion which she discovered from an early age. She loves reading books in her spare time.

The writer is a published author in two anthologies including an international #1 bestseller Train River Poetry Winter 2019 anthology with four more anthologies in pipeline.

Currently, she stays with her husband, Dr.Manish Kumar and two children in Warangal, Telangana.

To know more,

Follow her on Instagram at @anongirl146

 or

Mail her at vandana.pamulaparthy@gmail.com

CONTENTS

Seasons & Sun

Love & Lament

Illusions & Imagery

Life & Legacy

Dark & Desolate

Seasons

&

Sun

<u>Sunshine</u>

Charming, bright zeal

Of tulips, yellow

Scintillating exuberance

Of a morning sunshine

Rekindles a fire in me

That's long forgotten

Revives my hope

Of a promising tomorrow

<u>September Recipe</u>

The vibrant asters hue

Glory of the sapphire blue

Melody of the blue jay song

Mercurial rushes so strong

Virgin traits of sereneness

An aura of blissfulness

The autumnal equinox

Beauty of forget-me-nots

A perfect 'September recipe'

<u>Sagittarian Vibes</u>

A cold December night

With Sagittarian vibes

And romance in the air

We walk hand in hand

Sipping Hazelnut coffee

Those twinkles in your eyes

The hint of your smile

I keep blushing

Like a fool

It feels like a first date

Though I know it's not

Even when I forgot

Everything that we had

Dreams & Destiny

You didn't gave up

Trying to recreate

The magic we shared

You are making me

Fall in love with you

All over again!

I pray that it is for real

And not some vivid dream

<u>Summer Picnic</u>

(Six Squared Sam)

A summer day at Ashley's place

Lush, green orchards of sweet berries

Rich abundance of sun and play

Pies, cupcakes, fruit covered in glace

Stories of monsters, princes and fairies

Little girls picnic on their holiday

<u>Purple Haze</u>

The autumn chills

Are nudging me

Wrap me in your

Lucid trance

Embrace me with

Your smoky eyes

That emanate

A purple haze

Your mere presence

Is intoxicating

Liberate me with

Your tender warmth

First Snow

(Elfchen)

Winter

First snow

Soaring festive spirits

With shiny Christmas lights

Everywhere

The night

We first met

Kissing under the mistletoe

Dancing

Bodies swaying

In eternal mazes

Of warmth and desire

Hold

Comforting embraces

Intense passions unlocked

In sweet surrender of

Love

<u>Monsoon</u>

The monsoon brings along with it

A tinge of naughtiness

And a pinch of laziness

A plethora of magical trance

Peacock and its majestic dance

Little children and their paper boats

Colorful umbrellas and raincoats

Galloping rivers and boat races

Farmers and their happy faces

Proud tricolor flying in the sky

Sibling bonds soaring high

Splashes, giggles, hot pakoras

Coffee and delicious aromas

Augusts in India are special indeed

<u>Spring</u>

(Elfchen)

Spring,

Jubilant season

Enlivening nature's abundance

A reason to celebrate

Life

<u>Morning Glory</u>

Basking in the morning glory

I relish the first rays of sun

Embracing me warmly

In the early hours of dawn

Clinging to this enticing bliss

I look forward to a new start

A new hope, a new day

<u>Winter</u>

There they come

Covered in white cloaks

Howling in gusty winds

The very thought of them

Sends chills up my spine

While I lay sleepless

On those long, long nights

As if the scars in my heart aren't enough

They come to scar even my skin

Winters are truly cold

Love
&
Lament

<u>Journey of Love</u>

I first met you on that fateful night

For me it was love at first sight

You sat across from me sipping your tea

While I stole glances at you substantially

Our eyes met that spoke a hundred words

Together they travelled thousands of yards

We exchanged smiles filled with promises

Hopes of watching together million sunrises

An hour later you said 'Hi' and I replied 'Hi'

A beginning of our beautiful love story

And years later, I still do treasure

The train ticket that brought us together

<u>Symbol of Love</u>

Love is ubiquitous

Or so we think being hopeless romantics

We live for love, we live to love

And we love to live this way

A love so true, reflects in the eyes,

Gets etched into the folds of our minds

As memories to cherish forever

We find love everywhere,

In the first sprout emerged from a seed

In the first rain after scorching summer heat

The soft touch of a baby, blush of a young lady

Dew drops on the leaves, sunsets, and rainbows

Tempestuous Ocean, luminous full moon

Flowers, children, lovers, smiles from strangers

And so on.

We see the beauty in what we love

Or is it we love what is beautiful

Like the beautiful Taj Mahal

A monumental tomb built for love, out of love

So pristine that it is a universal symbol of love

No wonder that, it stands tall as a wonder of the world.

<u>Sapphire Nights</u>

Remember those days,

When we had all the time

In the world for each other

I wish we walk once again

Down the memory lane

And freeze the time forever

Where we watched sunsets together

As the sea waves played at our feet

Where we strolled down the beaches

Stealing kisses, in embraces tight

Where we erased our dark secrets

Turned them into lustrous lights

Where we explored each other in

Those sparkling sapphire nights

<u>Heartache</u>

I shall carve my love to you

In cryptic words with no clues

Entwine them into a fabric

Of the finest brocade blue

I shall then hide it in the

Darkest corner of a closet

Called your guilty conscience

Maybe, when you retrospect

And try to find my missing

Heart among your scattered

Leftovers of buried emotions

You'll know what heartache is

<u>Goodbye</u>

(Six Squared Sam)

Teary eyes, heavy heart, unknown anxiety

Goodbyes are too hard for me

Give a parting gift to remember

From January to end of December

A lasting hug or a lingering kiss

To year ahead that I miss

<u>Shattered Dreams</u>

(Six Squared Sam)

Promises broken, no hope to trace

Beliefs shaken, no plans to chase

Shattered my dreams, suppressed my voice

Regret pooled tears in my eyes

I can't live with your indifference

Moving on, I preserve my peace

<u>Broken Trust</u>

You befriended me to

Learn my secrets,

Play with my feelings

And to break me

You befriended me

When you needed help,

And after it is done

You didn't look back

You befriended me

To vent all your frustrations

And disappeared when I needed you

You used me and then trashed me

You broke my trust and betrayed me

I don't need friends like you

Instead of trusting someone like you

I've learnt to fight my battles alone

And celebrate my victories alone

<u>Find Me</u>

Find me in voids between our hearts

Find me in all your unspoken words

Find me in missed moments of endearment

Find me in failed promises and broken fulfillments

Find me in your feelings that you forgot to share

Find me in reflection of the mirror that you stare

Find me in your lies and my tears

Find me in my strengths and your fears

Find me in your fragile masculinity

Find me in the absence of our proximity

Try to find me in the time that got lost

Can you find me by renovating our past?

<u>Sacred Geometry</u>

At first, we were just two parallel lines

Traversing through different paths

Fate brought us together with an

Intersection of our love lines

Pretty soon, we jumped into a trajectory

Exchanging vows and rings

Expanding the radii of our circles

Merging both into a bigger one

Gradually, with passing of years

The shape of our love blossomed from

A familial triangle to a quadrilateral

Blessed we are tied to eternal bonds

By the strings of the sacred geometry

<u>**Unfulfilled Love**</u>

I walk towards the sands

Bare feet, empty-handed

Heart heavy with burden

Of the battered years

Pockets heavy with letters

Of old, tattered papers

That once contained many

Promises and hopes

Now, crumpled by the dried

Leaks of ink and my tears

Tonight when the red moon rises

I shall join the dancing ocean

To put an end to our unfulfilled love

<u>Pain of Rejection</u>

Loser

A failure

The black sheep

They call me names

And ignore me so blatantly

I cease to exist for them

They laugh behind my back

Seeing my battered soul

Ripped into pieces

As I

C

R

U

M

B

L

E

<u>Memories</u>

Though I have moved on

Your memories linger by

In the pages of my life

Just like this wrinkled flower

Between pages of my book

It's presence there but fragrance lost

<u>Love Never Hurts</u>

Love is a magical word

In an enchanting world

Love, in its varied manifestations

Cannot be defined wholly

To fall in love and be loved back

Is a bliss unconditionally

Love knows no boundaries;

Love is fearless

It is an eternal charisma

With feelings boundless

Love is everything and yet

A sweet nothing

Love is when you feel amazing,

Grateful and happy

It isn't love if you feel ashamed,

Guilty or helpless

If it hurts, it isn't love

Love is hope, not a doubt

Love is trust, not fear

Love is pride, not shame

If it hurts, it isn't love

Love is pleasure and love bites

Love is not pain and bruises

If it hurts, then it isn't love

It is power

It is poison

It is a game

If it hurts, then it isn't love

It is abuse

It is dominance

It is control

Because, love never hurts, my love!

I've Lost Myself

(Viator Poem)

I've lost myself

Abiding by their rules

Pleasing their whims

In a need for approval

Choking in shame

I've lost myself

As a pawn in their game

For fear of rejection

In their bigger picture of life

Overlooking my little things

I've lost myself

In building their dreams

Living in their shadows

I became a stranger to my own

To uncaring ways of the world

I've lost myself

<u>Heavy Heart</u>

You played with my heart

In the name of love

Broke it without a tint of guilt

Inflicting a pain so great

The emotional burden that I carry

Weighs too heavy on my shoulders

I wish I could lick all my concealed wounds

Pick all the pieces of my broken heart

Tie them together with a rope of hope

And wear it proudly on my back

For the world to see and learn

Though broken or damaged my heart is

It still beats so strong

Strong enough to leave behind

You and your miserable love

And embark on a new journey of life

<u>Angel from Heaven</u>

Withered by life's miseries

Abandoned in the cold

She was left to die

But then, he came along

An angel from heaven

To carry her to a safe abode

The fire in his eyes

Burned the icicles in her heart

The heat from his body

Warmed her frosty skin

As he held her in his sheltered arms

Blood rose to her cheeks

And, she came alive again

<u>A Needed Escape</u>

(Six Squared Sam)

Perched on a precipice of loneliness,

She ignored all her subconscious signs.

Distant dreams of hope beckoning her,

She donned ephemeral wings of fire.

A needed escape from harsh reality,

She took a leap of fatality.

<u>Swimming in Uncertainty</u>

The problem with me is

I love too much

I give too much

And when I can't get it back

My mind goes astray

In clouds of dismay

Hanging in between yes or no

Should I stay or just go

I need to know where I stand

Can't be a mere puppet in your hands

Maybe I scare you with my emotions

That you perceive as crazy notions

But, how long do I swim in uncertainty?

Before I get drowned by your insecurities

<u>Tomorrow</u>

(Lokhee Flip 4 poem)

Blazing flames burning in my heart

Raging pain, tearing me apart

Drowning in a sea of sorrow

I've lost all hopes of tomorrow

Why should I care for tomorrow?

When all it does bring is sorrow

I can't tell my senses apart

An unknown fear gripped my heart

Darling, once listen to your heart

It holds you from falling apart

When life is both joy and sorrow

Why are you scared of tomorrow?

A new light awaits tomorrow

That'll stray you away from sorrow

Come with me now, don't stay apart

I'll keep you lasting in my heart

Illusions

&

Imagery

<u>He Is Online</u>

He is online, says the little

Green dot on my screen

My heart speeds up with

A rush of Adrenaline

Not a lover, not a friend yet,

A stranger for now

But his very existence

Keeps me alive somehow

We sneak into the

Realm of words, undeterred

Apart from this world,

Yet a part of this world

I wish I were a fragment

Of his imagination

To be treasured forever

In the flair of his creation

<u>Traveler</u>

I am a traveler

Wandering in flights of fancy

I linger around engrossed

By all stories that I come across

I penetrate a little into

Each book that I read

Each song that I listen to

Every movie that I watch

Every person that I meet

Gathering a piece of their adventure

Interweaving them with my own

I live and lead many lives

In illusions of my mind

<u>Screaming Starlight</u>

Your butterfly kisses that flutter in my heart

Wild whispers of desire in screaming starlight

Touch of your lips on my sensual skin

Our passionate love in the name of sin

My world is spinning madly

Thoughts of you taunt me savagely

You left me tangled in time

Conjuring connections sublime

Fooling me yet again

In my dreams of smoke and rain

Say, it's real, not some magic trick

That has me craving for you sick

<u>**My Friends**</u>

When it is dusk

And I am lonely

My own shadow

Deserts me

I am aching for

Some company

And they come

To cheer me up

Perk my mood

Talk and laugh

Into the night

They are my

Only dear ones

I can never

Afford to lose

They are my

'Imaginary friends'

They keep me sane

In an insane world

<u>Colorful Pinball Poem</u>

(Parks Pinball Poem)

A colorful dream world

Coated in anomalies

Bright and bold

Silvers and gold

Glitters in the light

No plain black or white

Rainbows are lost

In tints of grays

Pink clouds float

In dark green skies

Sunflowers are blue

Raindrops a red hue

Dreams & Destiny

Purple elephants

Pandas with yellow pants

Orange tides of the seas

Cold indigo blood in my veins

Neon signs on trees

Watch out, please

Vibrant shades around you

Are made up, not true

Artificial is the new trend

Painting a vivid blend

In this dreamily colorful world

<u>Who Are You?</u>

Hush

A slip of your tongue

Might give away too much

Who knows what you hide

In your carefully crafted lies

The lies that you keep secured

Under lock and key in your attic

Ahem

A rip in your mask

May reveal your true face

That you try so hard to hide

With all those neatly arranged

Piles of masks in your closet

A range to choose for every occasion

Alas

Your basement's overflowing with

Archives of the secrets about to spill

That you've collected for years

Hidden beneath layers of coated dust

All the lies, masks and secrets

That makes up your life

What if they decide to

Break their shackles someday

And you begin to wonder

Who exactly are the real you?

<u>A Fantasy Land</u>

If there is an another world,

Called a land of fantasy

I'll take you there, my love

Where we live in golden castles

I'll be your prince, you be my princess

Where we'd ride unicorns that fly

And paint rainbows and clouds in the sky

Where we play catch with raindrops

Without a single concern nor care

With all the time in our hands

We shall live there forever

A life of fun and joy.

If there is an another world

A land that's real, not a fallacy

Please take me there, my love

Where there is no corruption

Crime, poverty or pollution

Neither racism nor honor-deaths

Where people are safe

With no fear of rape

Where humanity is the only religion

With compassion as its faith

We shall live there forever

A life of peace and love

Floral Bloom

(Triolet Poem)

Fragrance of the floral blooms

Alluring tangy intoxication

Fleeting aroma of exotic perfumes

Fragrance of the floral blooms

Bouquets of Lavenders, Orange blossoms

Magnolias, Jasmines and Carnations

Fragrance of the floral blooms

Alluring tangy intoxication

Visit to the Store

(Limerick)

I went to the store to buy some trout

Everyone there were laughing about

So, I picked up just eggs

And looked down my legs

To find that my pants are inside out

Tangled Mess

(Lokhee Colours Poem)

Like scattered stars in a dark midnight sky

My thoughts draped in black wings, they fly

Hovering above white streets of December

They search for you in all places they remember

In vast stretches of golden sand that surround

A carpet of blue sapphires glistening abound

The ocean's voice whispers our song of love

Silver breezes shower blessings from above

In the lush green wood that we walked together

I wait for you now dressed in silk and feather

Come, make me yours, and end my loneliness

Liberate me from my mind's tangled mess

<u>Books, Books and Books</u>

On a Midsummer night I had a dream

Alice gave me a key to the Wonderland

R. L. Stevenson mocked me not to

Confuse it with his Treasure Island

I was led into a tea party by Captain Nemo

Along with Twain, Verne, Dumas and Dickens

The Three Musketeers were laughing

As Sawyer and Copperfield chased chickens

Little Women were chatting with Mr. Darcy

Ayn Rand chanting, "Who is John Galt?"

The mighty Aslan with Edmund and Lucy

Watched squirrels hovering over Veruca Salt

I went further and found Hercule Poirot

Searching for lost King Solomon's Mines

"Let's ask Jeeves" suggested Wooster

As Chase and Archer sipped their wine

The Alchemist was talking to Dumbledore

About the magic of a Sorcerer's Stone

Harry, Ron and Hermione listening in

And the shepherd was standing far alone

Famished, I ate my fill at Hailey's Hotel

"It's the Day of the Jackal" Forsyth informed

Along came James Patterson's Spider

As "Big Little Lies" Moriarty exclaimed

Langdon was searching for his Lost Symbol

Doyle wanted us all to go to the Baker Street

So away we went with Gardner and Brown

Joined us were Perry Mason and Della Street

"It's all elementary" said Holmes to Watson

And suddenly everyone went into a Coma

"You should leave this Crisis" said Robin cook

"Go back to home, enough of this drama".

I staggered along to a melancholic air

Erich Segal was singing his sad Love Story

Sharing their 'Secrets' and 'Mistakes'

Amish and Bhagath strolled leisurely

I gave my key to the guard at my dream portal

"It's a password," said Sanghi "not Krishna Key"

"It's in a Testament in a Firm", mused Grisham

"Run away" whispered Coben "is the pass key"

"You have to go before Twilight sets in

When vampires and werewolves roam about,

Nothing Lasts Forever, even Best Laid Plans! "

Warned Sheldon as he ushered me out

Thus I woke up from my sleep

With books all around me in a heap

<u>Voices</u>

They call me sick

They call me mad

When, all I want is to help

Help to calm those voices

Voices! Voices!

I hear voices all the time.

They tell me it is all in my head

But I know whose voices are those

I hear the voice of wind when I am out driving

The flowers talk to me when I go for a walk

I hear the water speak to me when I shower

Birds, pets, babies and trees; I can hear them all

The voices speak to me in a rush

Sometimes they scream, sometimes a hush

Most of the time it is gibberish

But I hear the voices all the time

Sometimes I talk back to the voices

Either soothing them or scolding them

People look at me with fear

They call me insane

They call me mad

They call me sick

While, I am desperately trying to

Clear my head from their voices.

Life
&
Legacy

<u>Dreams and Destiny</u>

(Elfchen)

Dreams

Of mine

With fragile wings

Broke with a simple

Touch

Of a

Dark negative vibe

Hope they gain my

Trust

This time

And fly high

To reach their aimed

Destiny

<u>Kindness</u>

My parents taught me

To be always kind

That would, they said

Bring peace to my mind

What they never told me

Was that it comes with a price

Although kindness is often appreciated

At times, a virtue can be a vice

How much ever I love to

See smile on a folk's face

I hate it that much when they

Take me granted in their case

<u>Taste of Victory</u>

Her smile, an enthralling ecstasy

Her gait composed and confident

Her eyes sparkle with fervor

She exudes an aura of her own sunshine

She is invincible and unbreakable

A resilient spirit with a sanguine heart

She is all set to rule her world

Reveling in her first flush of victory

If there is an another world

A land that's real, not a fallacy

Please take me there, my love

Where there is no corruption

Crime, poverty or pollution

Neither racism nor honor-deaths

Where people are safe

With no fear of rape

Dreams & Destiny
Where humanity is the only religion

With compassion as its faith

We shall live there forever

A life of peace and love

<u>Wandering in The Wilderness</u>

Chaotic noises giving me jitters

Dusty air suffocating me

Rush of crowds with their litters

Their melancholies and urgency

I am trapped in a bubble so little

No space to breath, no place to move

Surviving this mayhem is a daily battle

This place is a jungle, by Jove!

And so when the wilderness beckoned me

With no second thoughts, I consented

The woods welcomed me heartily

Like a rebirth, I woke from dead

As fresh fragrance of breezes relaxed me

I lay down under the canopy of stars

While nature's music sang a lullaby

I slept like a baby on a bed of grass

With solace and warmth embracing me

Never have I felt this heavenly

This is how my 'home' should be

Mother nature herself my family

<u>The Girl Who Lost Her Smile</u>

Hey girl! Look at you

That scowl you are wearing

Has become a permanent

Feature of your face

You lost your smile

For a while now

Searching for happiness

In others' eyes

Everything you ever wished

Career, home, family

You have it all now

You are living

The dream

But the smile on your lips

Refused to replace

The frown of your brows

Dreams & Destiny
Harboring envy and bitterness

You forgot your true blessings

Checking out other people's lives

You ceased to live your own

<u>Silence</u>

Silence reigned most of my life

Though not by my choice

I ached to tell all my stories

Somehow couldn't find my voice

A fear of being misunderstood

Labeled my opinions as weak

An agony of myriad rejections

Subdued my desire to speak

The world called me a recluse

Accusing me of being distant

The irony was not lost on me

As loneliness had me vacant

Little do they know that initially

I set out to build bridges long

But ended up building a wall

That kept me hidden, safe and strong

<u>Nostalgia</u>

Good old times when we were little

You sat on your porch steps, smiling

And watched me play hopscotch

From across the street

Back then when we were neighbors

We walked to school together

Sharing jokes, candies, and giggles

Our faces ever bright

You grew your hair long, a wannabe rock star

We formed our little band and played music

On our pretend guitars, singing Bryan Adams'

Songs, in the moonlight

Now, we live in different time zones

Dreams & Destiny

Separated by vast oceans

Our paths never cross

We rarely chat

But, when I start to think of you,

My heart can't stop singing

"Those were the best days of my life."

<u>Let It Out</u>

Today try something different

Embrace yourself, for a change

Let go of your darkest fear

You deserve to be happy

More than you care

Let it out

Stop carrying the guilt

Or blame your being

Enough fighting with your

Inner demons

Vent all your frustrations

Let it out

Laugh aloud if it pleases you

Or cry your heart out

Do what it takes to heal you

Ignore the whispers and stares

Let it out

Dreams & Destiny
Don't be depressed, sweetheart

Nobody is perfect in this world

Release all your fears and doubts

Conquer all anxieties

Let it out

Don't hide those scars

Wear them with pride

Fall in love with self

Savor the essence of life

Let it out

If it scares you

That you are alone

I shall be there for you

Talk to me or walk with me

We'll face this together

But, darling, just this once

Let it all out

<u>Me Time</u>

The exquisite aroma of a

Chamomile and Calendula tea

From across the street

Stirred a dormant desire in me

When was the last time?

I hung out with friends

A day at a spa or a shopping spree

A slumber night or a movie date

It's been too long since I allowed

Myself a little luxury for leisure

Drowning in a hectic hi-tech life

I forgot to have my 'me time'

On a whim, I decide to take a day off

And pamper myself exclusively

No wonder that sometimes

Little unexpected things in life

Makes you realize the essence

Of what we are missing big time

<u>Motherhood</u>

Silent streams of alien emotions flooding

And clouding my clarity

Blaring screams of agony escape my lips

Stripping all my dignity

Soothing voices and hands held me back

Constraining me in captivity

Inevitable pain entwined with inordinate

Pleasure, shrugging off my sanity

And then, everything changed

For an everlasting moment

She cried and I cheered in unity

With her indigenous innocence,

An adorable angel adorned my arms

And I fell in love with her for eternity

Cherished Cage

My wings

Young and eager

Flutter with impatience

To fly far, far away

My roots

Old and strong

Hold on to me silently

Pleading not to leave

My mind

Quavering with qualms

Gloomy and uncertain

Settled for the roots

My heart

Trapped in bondages

With hidden pains and rages

Dreams & Destiny

Loses one more battle

But still beating strong

Time

Gradually and unconsciously

I relied more on my roots

I clipped both my wings

And I started to cherish

This cage, I call my home

<u>Introversion</u>

(Acrostic Poem)

I have a thousand monologues in my mind

Nine to ten times, I plan them all ahead

Totally useless as I get baffled yet again

Ranting to self, I babble like a bird-brain

Oh! I could have just stayed back home

Voicing my concerns to inanimate gnomes,

Embarrassed, I cringe at their lame jokes

Reason left me as I joined them folks

So, together we all share a laugh at my expense

Ideally, the conversation shifts to topics dense

Ostentatiously, I smile and nod at them to keep up

No wonder I want to get back to my haven from this trap

<u>Charm Bracelet</u>

My life dangles in those little charms

Their touch so gentle on my skin

Like dandelions dancing

To music of the wind

A sense of euphoria

My life dangles in those little charms

Vibrant trinkets around my wrist

Each with a story of its own

Each with a memory I hold close

A sense of nostalgia

My life dangles in those little charms

That adorns my pretty bracelet

A mingle of passions

A jingle of harmony

A sense of ataraxia

<u>Superheroes</u>

You worship superheroes

But do you realize

You are one too

Yeah! You are a superhero

With a bunch of superpowers

Hidden underneath your sleeve

Gratitude, compassion, charity

Practice your powers, cultivate them

They mold you into a better person

As you use them to heal people in need

And fight the super villains

Those are dwelling within you

Envy, pride and ego

Destroy them as you grow

Evolve into a superhero

Bury your monsters forever

And make our world

The best place to live in

<u>Her World</u>

His entry into her life was a big surprise

Totally unexpected

Her friends told her it was her call

To accept him or not

She somehow she knew that she had no choice

As he was already a part of her

His heart was beating within her

So, she decided to keep him

Her decision shocked people

Some cursed her, some ignored her

Few blamed her, most abandoned her

She didn't care what people thought

She only cared for him

She loved him with all her heart

Promised herself that she would never leave him

He might be a rape victim's son to the world

But to her, he is her whole world

<u>The Shakti</u>

She is

Paradigm of Femininity

Embodiment of Creation

Personification of Nature

She is

Quintessence of Beauty

Paragon of Confidence

Epitome of Knowledge

She is

Depiction of Positivity

Destroyer of Dark Evil

Protector of Harmony

She is

Symbol of Prosperity

Guardian of Morality

Dreams & Destiny
Preserver of Equality

She is

The Ultimate Energy

Of The Entire Universe

She is

The Shakti

The Goddess

<u>Where Has It Gone Wrong</u>

Her mere touch turned anything gold
Success followed her like a surname

Friends flocked around, never left her alone
They worshipped the ground that she trod

Her smile was enough to brighten their lives
She floated in the sea of their adorations

She danced to the music of their accolades
She was the queen, their chosen one

Well, she lost her Midas touch one day
A single failure curbed her celebrations

No spark in her to ignite smiles anymore
Friends deserted her, she's left all alone

She talks to herself in indistinct words
As she walks in circles on a barren ground

Desolated, she ponders endlessly in vain
Where has it all gone wrong?

<u>Woman</u>

You think she is fragile, weak or delicate

But, if you look into her psyche,

Walk in her shoes for a day

You'll know she is 'The Strength'

The force that runs the world

She hovers above like a sky

(That can drop you)

With the patience of Mother Earth

(That can shake you)

She flexes her spirit like water

(That can drown you)

She adapts to her milieu like air

(That can hurl you)

Housing fire inside her soul

(That can burn you)

She has added strength to destroy you,

If she chose to

But, her innate ability lies in creation,

Not destruction

Who is she, but a woman, embracing the elements of the nature
within her?

<u>Self Love</u>

Mirror, mirror on the wall

I know I am not the fairest of all

Pray tell me how to stand tall

I fear of rising back after a fall

Pretty damsel, truth be told

Fair is the love that a heart holds

All that glitters is not gold

Stand up with your stance bold

Wear shoes made for prominence

Head high, walk with confidence

What matters is your attitude

Adamancy mingled with gratitude

Life is both sun and rain

A blend of pleasures and pain

Don't see me as just another face
I am not your rival in any case

Look into you through my eyes
You'll see you are fair in all sense

<u>Fly High</u>

They'll tell you

You are doing it wrong

They accuse you

On not being strong

They'll laugh at you

When you fall

They won't answer

Your frantic calls

They try to teach you

To remain insignificant

They'll preach you that

It's a sin to be independent

No matter what they do or say

Dreams & Destiny

You are what you believe in

97

Don't let them confine you

Within the walls of their insecurities

Darling, you are born to be free

So, adorn the wings of your choice

And fly high until you reach your purpose

<u>Roses Are Red</u>

Roses are red

We talk about women empowerment

But we are still helpless

Watching girls get raped and killed

Roses are red

We talk about awareness of mental health

But we are still clueless

For hundreds of unexplained suicides

Roses are red

We talk about love and peace

But we are still hopeless

Fighting wars both without and with bloodshed

Roses are red

We always judge people around us

But we are all hypocrites

Praising the same people once they are dead

<u>Life of Paradoxes</u>

She assures herself she's okay though, broken to the core

Donning a mask of radiance as she opens her doors

She stands as an epitome of an elite lifestyle

Wearing a bright orange dress and a glowing smile

Surrounded by people, in a picture larger than life

She thinks of times she almost cut her wrists with a knife

Little do they know that she is in shatters

Fighting demons in dark alleys of her grey matter

She soothes all her friends and wipes their tears

But none of them knows she hides her own dark fears

She gives out love and affection that she craved

Embracing the heavy pain that has her enslaved

They can't comprehend the gloom consuming her heart

She's always been lonely from the very start

They go green with envy seeing the pink of her cheeks

While her bleeding soul finds no solace that she seeks

They think they fool her by posing as her thick friends

But she tricks them back by pretending that she blends

She knows to fight her battles alone by being brave

And conceal her painful secrets to take them to the grave

<u>Think Of Me</u>
<u>(Viator Poem)</u>

Think of me and I'll be there

When you feel life's leading nowhere

I may not open new doors for you

But I'll hold your hand as you pour out your heart

When days just seem to pass in a blur

Think of me and I'll be there

I'll share your burdens and woes

And entertain you with my crude jokes

When everything seems to fall apart

Nothing good is happening at all

Think of me and I'll be there

I promise to bring a smile on your face

Dreams & Destiny

When you seem to lose all hopes

You wish you had someone back you

When you're tired of being so brave for long

Think of me and I'll be there

Dark
&
Desolate

<u>Seduction of A Succubus</u>

I fell prey to a succubus seduction

On the night of a hunter's moon

Her touch burned my skin like fire

Her kiss as fatal as a vampire bite

She lured me with a song of a siren

To the gallows of an abandoned prison

I lost the war within my insane mind

Walked right into her gripping arms

And in her perilous love

Death became me

<u>Life After Death</u>

In my mind, I've always wondered

How life would be after death.

Will there be hell and heaven?

Or just a medium filled with light?

Will I meet other souls?

Are they friendly or do we fight?

Will people shed tears for me?

Will my loved ones really miss me?

Can I be able to see them?

Would they able to sense me?

How would I know my death is near?

So I can be well-prepared.

I wish I could write my journey to death

For people curious to read.

As I spend my sleepless nights pondering over death,

My heart gently reprimands me

"Why do you waste time on uncertainty?

While you are alive now

Make memories, laugh and love

For this life is not going to last forever".

<u>Little Angel, Rest in Peace</u>

You were daddy's girl and mommy's world

Your dimpled smiles were precious treasures

Your little squeals were music to their ears

You were the future, baby girl,

A hope they looked upon to

But, the day that you left them

Their world just shattered apart

The monster that had hidden in your closet

Was a fictitious creature no more

That night, he came alive, a bloody brutal beast

To rip off your tender innocence

He broke your fragile soul,

Trapped you with his mighty strength,

And left you all bruised and bleeding

The world stopped for a minute or two

To mourn for the merciless deed

Oh darling! You were too little

To even know that a crime was being committed

All the tears, the prayers,

The protests for justice,

Was all that (not) enough, sweetheart?

What more could we, helpless humans,

Have done to bring you back to this world?

This cruel place down here is hell

Dear little angel! Rest in peace in heaven

<u>Haunting Eyes</u>

Walking away from you

When you needed me the most

I am not proud of myself

Now, I sit all alone by the window

Watching the September moon

With a drink in my unsteady hands

With flickering mind, heart beating fast

I pick up your picture one last time

My cowardly eyes hesitate to look

At your piercing, blazing eyes

Ah! Those eyes that are burning me

Haunting me, turning me into a wreck

I am filled with guilt as I turn away from

Those eyes that accuse me of being alive

While they lay, lifeless in a buried grave

<u>In The Dark</u>

We have always lived in the castle

Unknown to any human soul

Where birds flew in magic swirls

In the darkest of dark skies

We've lost the meaning of time

Waiting for the moon to unveil

The burden of secrets hidden

Deep beneath the blue seas

We hope in vain to be rescued

From this gloomy, doomed land

Blinded, we wish for a miracle

For light ceased to exist in us

<u>The Little Stranger</u>

On a day as warm as my skin

I first saw the little stranger

Standing near a witch hazel tree

Its leaves falling at his feet

He was dressed in a loose garb

Seemingly made of raven feathers

His eyes were leering bloody red

His hair covered in spider webs

The sight of him kept haunting me

For days together, until today

When I saw him again at my door

Waiting to prey on my blood

Even before I got a chance to run

He pounced upon me like a tiger

As he pinned me down like a doll
An evil smile played on his lips

And just before he snapped my neck
He whispered in a hoarse tone

"All humble beginnings have to
Suffer miserable endings."

<u>October Creeps</u>

Ancestral wounds that run so deep

Ghosts from the past around me weep

Sounds from under the bed never let me sleep

Whispers of the October winds that creep

Eerie alchemical vibes silently peep

I am a fallen angel with secrets to keep

Monster Under My Bed

(Tail Twister Poem)

There, I hear them again

Is it real or is it my dream?

A hoarse whisper and an eerie laugh

Monster lurking around in the dark

Under my comforter, I lay trembling

My heart beats loud in the heavy silence

Bed spread of mine gets pulled away

Or is it my legs that are being pulled

Maybe I am going to be dead tonight

It's my last night on this Earth

Just how much longer will I be alive?

In my last seconds, I wished I met them all

My friends and family, for one last time before, I

Head off into the nether regions of hell

There is a monster under my bed

Or maybe it's just in my head

<u>Empty Tunnels</u>

I saunter sometimes

On lonely nights

Into empty tunnels

With flickering lights

Wailing walls of which

Sing a sad melody

Grieving ghosts linger

About in melancholy

Intrigued by their stories

From another lifetime

That got lost somewhere

In tracks of time

I help them get through

The limbo of darkness

As a little gesture

Of my emphatic kindness

Followed By Death

(Tricube Poem)

I see him

Following

All the way

He stays near

But hidden

In shadows

Dark hearted

Grim reaper

Soul eater

<u>Dark Dreams</u>

(Haiku)

Deciduous dreams

Desperately drenched down in

Dark, destitute drains

<u>Appendix</u>

These are some of the poetic forms that I had a chance to write in.

1. *<u>Acrostic Poem</u>*

Acrostic poetry is where the first letter of each line spells a word, usually using the same words as in the title.

2. *<u>Elfchen</u>*

Elfchen is a German poetic form consisting of eleven words in a specific format of words per line:
Row 1: one word
Row 2: two words
Row 3: three words
Row 4: four words and
Row 5: one word.

3. *<u>Haiku</u>*

Haiku is a very short Japanese poetry form composed of three unrhymed lines of 5, 7 and 5 syllables.

4. *Limerick*

A Limerick is a rhymed humorous or nonsense poem of five lines which originated in Limerick, Ireland. The Limerick has a set rhyme scheme of: a-a-b-b-a with a syllable structure of: 9-9-6-6-9.

5. *Lokhee Colours Poem*

This form is created by the Australian author and poet Linda Lokhee.

The poem contains 3 stanzas with rhyming pattern AaBb with 10 syllables in each line.

There should be two colors in stanza 1, three colors in stanza 2 and one color in stanza 3.

6. *Lokhee Flip Four Poem*

This poetic form is also created by Australian author and poet Linda Lokhee.

The poem should contain four stanzas with 2 rhyming couplets per stanza and 8 syllables per each line. Each stanza should use the same end words but reversed (flipped around) in the next stanza. Linda is an Instagram user with id @lindalohkeeauthor.

7. *Parks Pinball poem*

This poem contains a minimum of 20 lines that starts with a simple phrase for the first line and then it should be free associated by any idea that comes to mind from the sound, words or concept of that line. The first line should be related to the last by a matching word. The poem title should contain words from the first and last line along with the words 'parks, pinball or pinball poem'.

This poetry form is created by an Instagram user Elaine with id @twisted.word.tango.

8. *Roses are Red*

The poem should start with the line Roses are red. It is created by the Instagram user with id @roses.are.rob.

9. *Six Squared Sam*

This is a poem containing six lines of six words each (total 36 words). Each line should exist on its own as a 6 word poem. Combined with other lines, it forms a longer cohesive poem. Rhyming of the end word is either Aa/Bb/Cc or ABC/abc.
This form is created by Instagram user Sam with id @colourful_anomaly.

10. *Tail twister Poem*

In this poem, the last line must be made up of all the first words of all the preceding lines in the order they appear and they must twist or invert the mood

Rhyming is optional. This form is created by the Instagram user with id @randomerbobsxyz.

11. *Tricube Poem*

It is a mathematical poetic form created by Phillip Larrea. The poem contains three stanzas. Each stanza contains three lines. Each line contains three syllables.

12. *Triolet Poem*

A Triolet is a poetic form consisting of only 8 lines. Within a Triolet, the 1st, 4th, and 7th lines repeat, and the 2nd and 8th lines do as well. The rhyme scheme is ABaAabAB, capital letters representing the repeated lines.

13. *Viator Poem*

The viator form was invented by Canadian author and poet, Robert Skelton. It consists of any stanzaic form in which first line of the first stanza is the second line of the second stanza and so on until the poem ends with the line with which it began.